How Do Ladybugs Get Their Spots?

Written and Illustrated by

Elizabeth Adams Burchell

ISBN 978-1-64468-634-8 (Paperback)
ISBN 978-1-64468-635-5 (Digital)

Covenant Books, Inc.
11661 Hwy 707
Murrells Inlet, SC 29576
www.covenantbooks.com

To my mother, Shirley Adams, who has always believed in me and is the reason this book is published. I am the woman I am today because of her amazing love and faith. There is no doubt she is my hero.

Once upon a time, there lived a baby bug named Lola. Lola was the youngest of her family and was very different from her brothers and sisters. She had no spots!

2

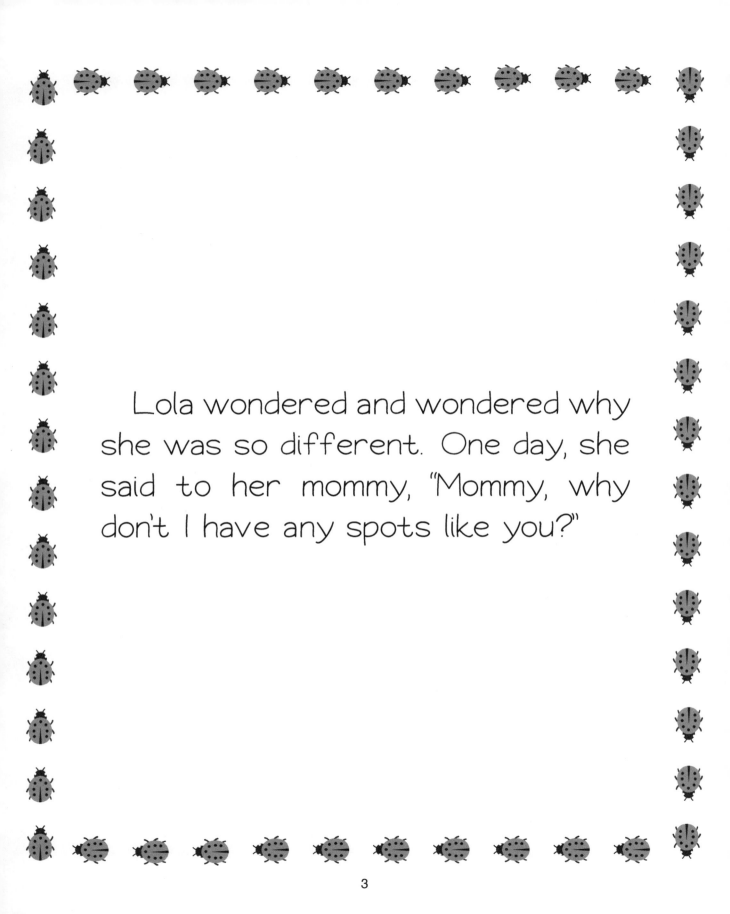

Lola wondered and wondered why she was so different. One day, she said to her mommy, "Mommy, why don't I have any spots like you?"

Her mommy said to her, "Well, Lola, you have to earn them."

Lola looked at her mommy with a puzzled face and said, "How do I do that?"

Mommy ladybug replied, "You see, Lola, as a baby bug grows into a ladybug, she has to learn many things. She has to learn to be polite and to say please and thank you. She has to learn to share. She has to learn to keep herself clean and always wash her hands before eating, and she has to learn to be trustworthy and honest."

Later on that day, Lola was playing with her doll bugs, and she called to her mommy, "Mommy, may I please have some bug juice?"

"Yes, you may, Lola, come and get it!"

"Thank you."

After Lola was finished with her bug juice, she went outside to have a picnic. Along came her friend, Herby. He looked very sad. Lola said to him, "Do you want to play with me? You can hold my doll bug!"

"Oh, great!" said Herby.

"Lola, Lola, it's time for dinner."
Lola hurried inside and headed straight for the bathroom. *Never forget to wash your hands,* she remembered as she washed her face and combed her hair.

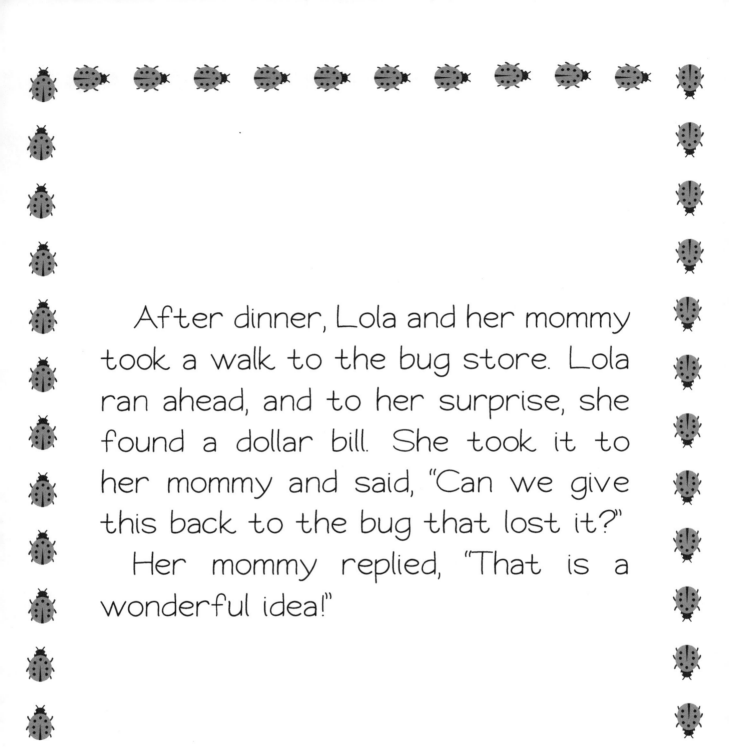

After dinner, Lola and her mommy took a walk to the bug store. Lola ran ahead, and to her surprise, she found a dollar bill. She took it to her mommy and said, "Can we give this back to the bug that lost it?"

Her mommy replied, "That is a wonderful idea!"

Bedtime came, and her mommy tucked her in. "Sweet dreams, Lola. See you in the morning."

18

As the sun shone into her room, Lola awoke, and to her surprise, she found what she had been waiting for. "Mommy, Mommy, look at me! I have spots, just like you!"

About the Author

Elizabeth Burchell lives in Richmond, Virginia, with her three busy children and supportive husband.

She teaches third-grade math, science, and history at a local elementary school. She originally wrote this story when she was a senior in high school over eighteen years ago.

CPSIA information can be obtained
at www.ICGtesting.com
Printed in the USA
LVHW071824120821
695159LV00007B/201